My Sister Beth's Pink Birthday

A Story About Sibling Relationships

In memory of my mother Regina who inspired this story and
who continues to inspire me every day.—*MLS*

To Romane, Marine, and Sophie, my 3 beautiful nieces.—*CB*

Published by
Magination Press
An Educational Publishing Foundation Book
American Psychological Association
750 First Street, NE
Washington, DC 20002

For more information about our books, including a complete catalog, please write to us, call 1-800-374-2721,
or visit our website at www.apa.org/pubs/magination.

Printed by Phoenix Color Corporation, Hagerstown, MD
Book design by Gwen Grafft

Library of Congress Cataloging-in-Publication Data

Szymona, Marlene L.
  My sister Beth's pink birthday : a story about sibling
relationships / by Marlene L. Szymona, PhD ; illustrated by
Christine Battuz.
      pages cm
  "American Psychological Association."
  Summary: "A picture book that aims to help young
children deal with the issue of sibling rivalry and
sharing within the context of a birthday celebration"—
Provided by publisher.
  ISBN-13: 978-1-4338-1654-3 (hardcover)
  ISBN-10: 1-4338-1654-7 (hardcover)
  ISBN-13: 978-1-4338-1655-0 (pbk.)
  ISBN-10: 1-4338-1655-5 (pbk.)
 [1. Sibling rivalry—Fiction. 2. Sharing—Fiction.
3. Sisters—Fiction. 4. Birthdays—Fiction.] I. Battuz,
Christine, illustrator. II. Title.
  PZ7.S998My 2014
  [E]—dc23
              2013048299

Manufactured in the United States of America
First printing April 2014
10 9 8 7 6 5 4 3 2 1

My Sister Beth's Pink Birthday
A Story About Sibling Relationships

by Marlene L. Szymona, PhD

illustrated by Christine Battuz

My sister Beth turns three today.
I am six.

Beth is still a baby.
But Mom says she is a little girl now.

I go to a red brick school.
But Beth stays home.
That's when she plays with Sam.
Sam is my stuffed pink bunny.

I tell her no!

He is mine.

Mom says we should share.

But Mom also says some toys can be just for me.

I hide Sam so Beth can't play with him.

Today Mom asked me to help her bake a cake with pink icing.
I love pink icing.
So now Beth likes it too.
Mom lets us both lick the icing from the green bowl.
Our fingers turn pink.

Beth likes what I like.
That makes her a baby.
But Mom says Beth just wants to be like me.
So I have to be good.
I think Beth is too little for cake.

Dad comes home from work.
He has a big pink box.
Is it for me?
No, he hands it to Beth!

Now Grandma walks in.
She has a huge pink box.
She puts it in Beth's arms.

Then Aunt Ann comes.
She has a pink box with sparkles on it.
It must be for me.
No. She gives it to Beth!

Next Uncle Dan rings the bell.
He hands me a present.
Then he points to a pink bike with
a basket and a bell.
It is hidden in the bush outside.
He says it is a secret.
It must be for me.
Beth sits at the head of the table.

They all sing happy birthday to Beth.
I won't sing.
Mom frowns at me.
Beth tries to blow out three candles.

But one is left.
I try to help her.
But Dad says, "Jen, let Beth do it."

Beth starts to open her gifts.

Mom and Dad got Beth a pink
ballerina dress and pink shoes.
I think she is too young for a
ballerina dress and shoes.

Next Beth opens the box from Grandma.
She pulls out a Barbie doll with a pink gown.
I think Beth is too little for a Barbie.
Beth opens the box from Aunt Ann.

Wow, a pink teddy bear!
I go to pet it.
But Aunt Ann says, "no, Jen."
Now it is time for my bike!

Uncle Dan wheels it in.
But he stops in front of Beth.
He says, "Happy birthday," and gives her a hug.

Oh, Uncle Dan says he has a gift for me!
He hands me a little pink bag.
I pull out a book about frogs.

It's the same one Mom bought me last year.
I yell, "Frogs are gross!"
I go to my room.

Soon all the guests go home.
I sneak down to the chair where all the presents are.
Then, I quietly take the gifts upstairs to my room.

The bike is hard to move.
It has three wheels on the back.
So I hide it in the bush.

From my room I hear Beth cry.
"Where are my gifts?
My gifts are all gone," she sobs.

Then Mom comes in.
The doll and bear are on my bed.
I have put on the dress and shoes.
But they are tight.

Mom sits next to me.
She smiles and kisses me on the head.
"Jen, why do you have Beth's gifts?"
I tell her Beth is too little for these things.
She is a baby.

But Mom says, "Beth loves her gifts.
And they are hers."
"But what about me?" I ask Mom.

"Your birthday is next month, remember?
Today is Beth's birthday.
Next month we will do something special for you."
Mom hands me a small pink bag.

Inside are party favors Beth saved for me.
I pull out pink candies and a bottle of bubbles.
And there is a cool picture Beth made.
She drew us holding hands.
And we are blowing pink bubbles.

Beth stands at the door. "Jen, you found the presents!
Thank you for keeping them safe.
You can play with the toys if you want.
We can play together. And we can share."
I didn't take the presents to keep them safe.

Is Beth a baby if she knows how to share?
I decide to get Sam from under my pillow.
I hand the bunny to Beth and say, "Happy pink birthday, Beth."
She says, "I love this present the best, and I love you."
Beth hugs me.

I hug Beth back.
And she does not feel like a baby at all.

Note to Parents and Other Caregivers

Parents and other caregivers can play an important role in helping siblings get along. In fact, the earlier you provide opportunities for your children to develop a positive sibling relationship, the more likely they will be to maintain those bonds and benefit from the many lessons they learn. You may have dealt with a bossy older brother, taken care of a younger sister, or been everyone's favorite only brother. The truth is that while there are a number of factors that make each family unique—including birth order, gender, age, spacing, temperament, family size, and parenting style—rivalry is a common issue between siblings. The good news is that there are a number of concrete steps you can take to smooth out disputes and develop positive sibling relations.

How This Book Can Help

Reading this book together with your child will provide an opportunity for her to ask questions and provide input. Note your child's reactions and feelings. Explaining that a younger sibling has needs similar to her own can move your child out of "me-only" thinking. Before reading this story, tell your child to ask questions whenever one comes to mind. During or after reading the story together, here are some sample questions you might ask your child:

- "Why do you think Jen won't sing 'Happy Birthday'?"
- "Why do you think Jen thinks the bike is for her?"
- "Why did Uncle Dan bring Jen a book?"
- "What do you think about Jen's decision to take the presents up to her room?"
- "Why did Jen decide to give Sam to Beth?"

Ideas for Improving Sibling Relationships

Set rules for sibling disputes. Before you attempt to settle any dispute between your children, consider if it might be better if they figure things out on their own. Children can learn valuable lessons by trying to resolve conflicts. However, be sure there are rules in place for settling disputes. You may want to include your children in setting up such guidelines since a more democratic parenting style can result in better sibling interactions. Ask your children what they think some rules could be. For example, hitting and name-calling should not be tolerated and consequences should be enforced with consistency.

Discuss how the other sibling might feel. Younger children will need more guidance in dealing with disputes, but they will learn valuable skills working out problems with your help. Parents need to help the older sibling understand how the younger child feels. For example, you could ask the older child how she thinks her younger brother or sister feels when someone pulls a toy away. Or you might ask, "How do you think your sister will like the present we bought? Why do you think so?" Often, older siblings may resent imitation, so you would be providing a new perspective by saying, "your sister wants to imitate you because she looks up you, admires, and loves you so much. As she gets older, she will have her own interests."

Validate all feelings. Let your children express all their feelings and ask them to explain why they think they reacted in a certain way. You might say something like, "These feelings are really natural, and everyone has them from time to time." Ask for positive suggestions that would improve the situation and make them feel better. For example, you might say, "I used to feel this way with my older sister sometimes until we decided that some toys would be just ours alone, and others would be for sharing." Don't punish children for their honesty, and compliment them when they explain feelings well. For instance, "You explained that very well so I now really understand exactly how you feel and what made you react this way."

Plan activities siblings can do together. Suggesting creative, fun, and non-competitive activities for your children to engage in together is a wonderful way to help build strong sibling bonds and make memories that can last a lifetime. Helping prepare a meal together; planning and putting on a puppet show or play; collaborating on a collage; or playing office, store, school, or even talk show host (in which siblings switch roles from time to time) are just some of the activities that teach children to collaborate naturally.

Treat siblings as individuals. Never compare children. Treat them as individuals with their own strengths and interests. Oftentimes, severe competition results from siblings choosing a sport or school activity because a brother or sister has. Discuss with your children why they chose a certain activity and what their other options are. You might ask, "Since you enjoy swimming so much, have you considered the swim team?" Or, "Have you thought about joining the choir since it can help you further develop your great music skills?" Younger children may find it difficult to compete academically with an older gifted sibling, so they sometimes decide to be different by not focusing on schoolwork. Tell your children, "School is a priority, and everyone can do well, even if you have other interests too." Having older siblings mentor or tutor younger ones can often be helpful as well.

Aim for fairness. Try to see situations from your children's point of view. Many times an older sibling may resent the increased time you spend with a younger sibling, and younger siblings may resent the privileges older siblings receive. In this case, you may explain by saying something like, "When your brother was your age, he went to bed at eight, and when you are older, you can stay up later too." You might also add that with age comes increased responsibility. For example, "You have more chores since you are older and can handle more. At his age, your younger brother needs to focus on cleaning up his room." Since sibling rivalry is often about attention, try to make sure you spend some alone time which each child, focusing on unique interests. You might, for example, take your daughter to the art museum and your son to the animal shelter. You could take each to the library, but at different times.

Be a positive role model. Modeling loving relationships and remaining positive and complimentary is perhaps the most important thing a parent can do to foster healthy sibling connections. How you interact with your spouse, siblings, and friends will be part of your children's early lessons in relationships. Tell children stories about you and your siblings, fun things you did together, as well as conflicts and how you resolved them. Compliment positive behaviors by saying something like, "It's wonderful how you and your brother worked so well together on that skit. You blended each other's suggestions to make something so much bigger and better than you might have created alone."

Rivalry is a natural part of growing up with siblings, and many valuable lessons are learned when siblings interact. However, if at any time rivalry becomes out of control or is too much to handle, it may be helpful to consult a licensed psychologist or other mental health professional. Relationships between siblings will change as individuals mature, move away, and have diverse experiences. However, providing a strong foundation can help the bond between siblings survive a lifetime.

About the Author

Marlene L. Szymona, PhD, has been telling stories since she was a little girl. Now retired, she decided to take her friends' and colleagues' suggestion to finally write and publish some of these stories. Based on an actual event, this is her first children's book. Dr. Szymona was born in New Jersey, and spent much of her adult life in Boston, then North Carolina. She received her doctorate in Curriculum and Instruction from the University of North Carolina at Chapel Hill. She has taught professional writing and composition at a number of universities, including North Carolina State University. She recently moved to the St. Petersburg area where she writes, reads, walks on the beach, and enjoys local theater and music.

About the Illustrator

Christine Battuz obtained a Master of Arts degree from l'Ecole de Beaux Arts de Perugia in Italy. Her delightful illustrations can be found in about forty children's books and magazines.

About Magination Press

Magination Press is an imprint of the American Psychological Association, the largest scientific and professional organization representing psychologists in the United States and the largest association of psychologists worldwide.